The Magical Elements

Written and Illustrated by

Anesha Penigar

AuthorHouse™
1663 Liberty Drive
Bloomington, IN 47403
www.authorhouse.com
Phone: 833-262-8899

Because of the dynamic nature of the Internet, any web addresses or
links contained in this book may have changed since publication and
may no longer be valid. The views expressed in this work are solely those
of the author and do not necessarily reflect the views of the publisher,
and the publisher hereby disclaims any responsibility for them.

Any people depicted in stock imagery provided by Getty Images are
models, and such images are being used for illustrative purposes only.
Certain stock imagery © Getty Images.

This book is printed on acid-free paper.

ISBN: 978-1-6655-1032-5 (sc)
ISBN: 978-1-6655-1033-2 (e)

Library of Congress Control Number: 2020924277

Print information available on the last page.

Published by AuthorHouse 12/07/2020

authorHOUSE®

Dedicated to:

My joyous, kind, smart, and beautiful daughter Judayah. I love you and thank you for pushing me to be a better mom.

In the beginning of time there were three elements that made up our beautiful world, the moon, the stars, and the sun. These three magical rays of light were governed by three goddesses: Moonlight, Starbright, and Sunbeam. They kept all three elements moving in time and space so that there would be life on earth. Moonlight balanced the moon on her feet while keeping it aligned with the sun, Sunbeam held the sun over her head while absorbing its hot temperatures, and Starbright tasseled each star to its perfect position to guide those lost. These three goddesses kept everything aligned and balanced within our universe.

One day there became great darkness and all three elements of our universe disappeared. Each was stolen and hidden away for great evil. Moonlight, Starbright, and Sunbeam had to find each magical ray of light before everything in our universe would be gone forever. There was a God named Pilfer, known for traveling in time stealing key elements to harvest for power. Pilfer has hidden each magical ray of light in a place where the goddesses didn't have permission to go, Earth. If the sun, moon, and stars aren't found before Pilfer harvests their powers time will be at a standstill and all things would vanish.

The goddesses had to get permission from the God Almighty to go to Earth and find the missing elements of life. Once permission was granted all three goddesses would be sent to Earth in human form for twenty-four hours. In disguise Moonlight, Starbright, and Sunbeam went their separate ways in search for the magical rays of light.

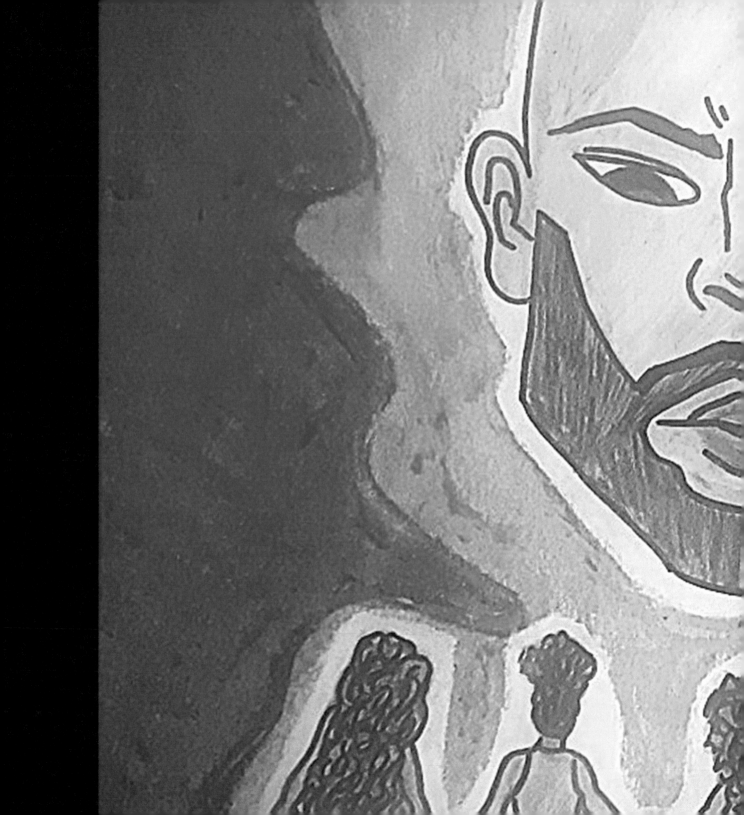

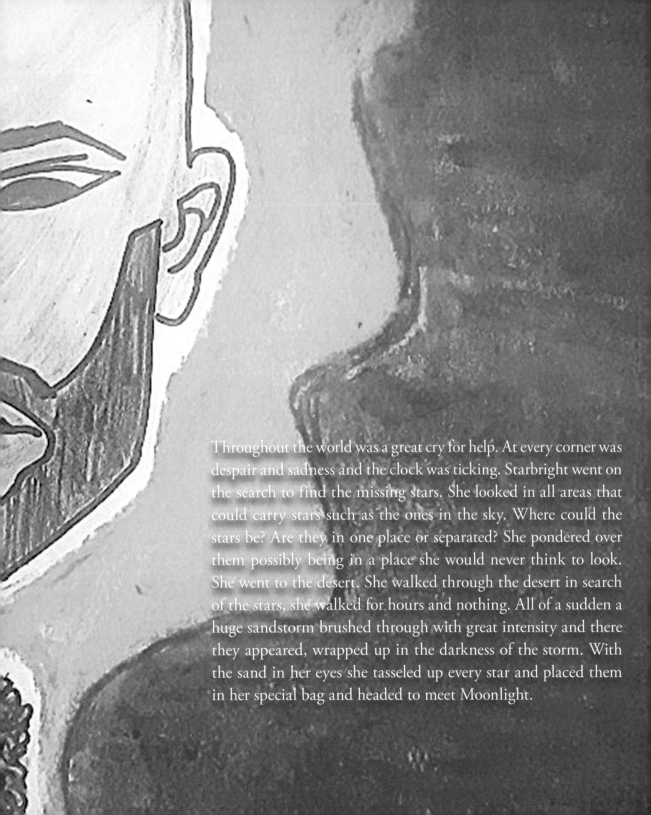

Throughout the world was a great cry for help. At every corner was despair and sadness and the clock was ticking. Starbright went on the search to find the missing stars. She looked in all areas that could carry stars such as the ones in the sky. Where could the stars be? Are they in one place or separated? She pondered over them possibly being in a place she would never think to look. She went to the desert. She walked through the desert in search of the stars, she walked for hours and nothing. All of a sudden a huge sandstorm brushed through with great intensity and there they appeared, wrapped up in the darkness of the storm. With the sand in her eyes she tasseled up every star and placed them in her special bag and headed to meet Moonlight.

The goddess Moonlight searched far and wide for the moon. She searched through the mountains, through the depths of valleys, through the darkest caves, but wait she was missing something. She noticed that there was a disruption in all sources of water. She went to the largest ocean and noticed there was a gravitational pull that caused massive waves and disturbance in all life forms. She needed to get to the bottom of the ocean, but how? Moonlight began to meditate to harness the power of the moon's magnetic and gravitational pull. The moon acted as a magnet and pulled her towards it with great force. As she floated above the moon she had to figure out how she was going to get it back into the sky.

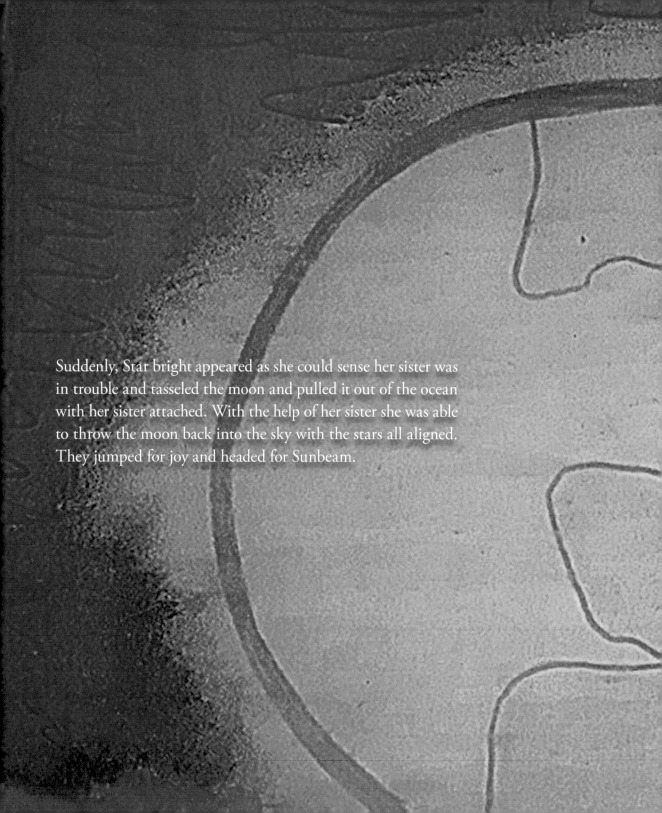

Suddenly, Star bright appeared as she could sense her sister was in trouble and tasseled the moon and pulled it out of the ocean with her sister attached. With the help of her sister she was able to throw the moon back into the sky with the stars all aligned. They jumped for joy and headed for Sunbeam.

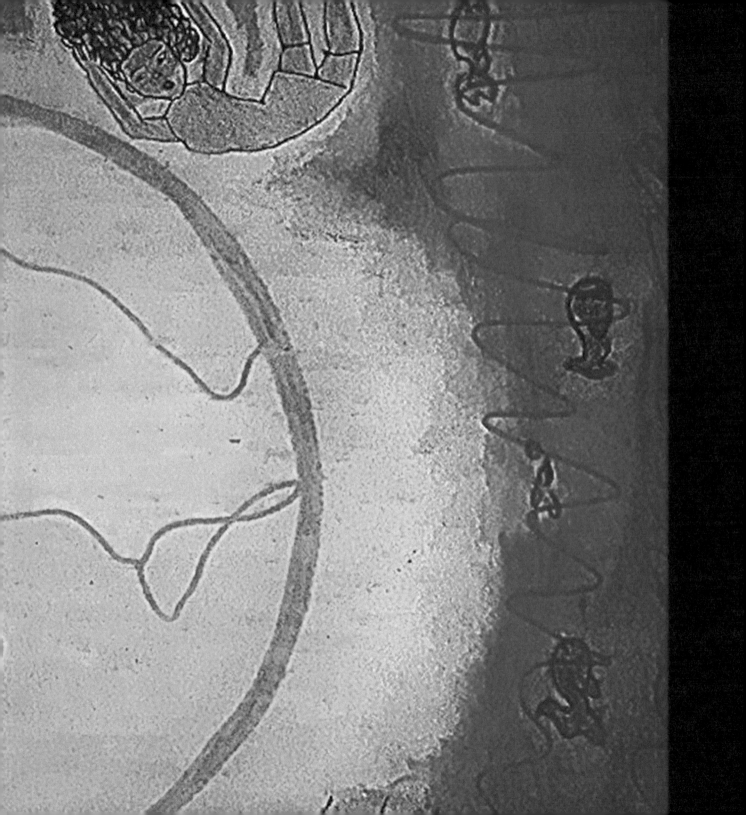

The goddess Sunbeam had been searching all day for the sun. She travelled to the biggest volcanoes and stood over the top and looked inside of each one and no sun. She kept searching, she checked the hottest places on earth and still no sun. Sunbeam thought to herself there are only a couple places the sun could be to harness such power and heat. She headed to the equator and planted herself right on the line, as she stood there she could feel a vibration underneath her feet. Sunbeam thought to herself what if the sun was inside the earth. She used the powers that she absorbed from the sun to make a hole in the center of the earth, just then a great beam of light shot out from the center of the earth up towards the sky. She found the sun!

She had to figure out a way to retrieve it. The only way was to absorb as much as she could without killing herself. She needed her sisters to help her balance the energy within the sun. Just in time Moonlight and Starbright reached Sunbeam as she was absorbing as much as she could to contain the sun's massive energy. They had to help her before the sun would kill her. With Moonlight's magnetic pull to harness energy she helped Sunbeam position her energy into something that would reflect the light and reduce the amount of energy put out. She placed herself in the ocean and Starbright used her tassel to pull Sunbeam in a direction to lift the sun out of the center of the earth and throw it back into the sky.

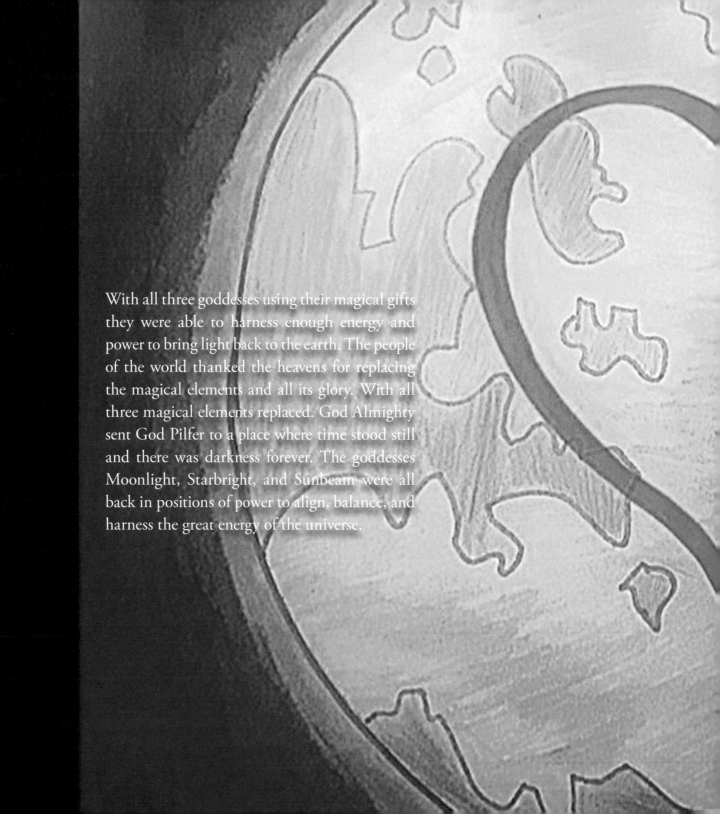

With all three goddesses using their magical gifts they were able to harness enough energy and power to bring light back to the earth. The people of the world thanked the heavens for replacing the magical elements and all its glory. With all three magical elements replaced. God Almighty sent God Pilfer to a place where time stood still and there was darkness forever. The goddesses Moonlight, Starbright, and Sunbeam were all back in positions of power to align, balance, and harness the great energy of the universe.

The End

Printed in the United States
By Bookmasters